twenty-four!). Helena lives in Nottinghamshire with

her husband and has two grown-up children.

The Girls FC series

Do Goalkeepers Wear Tiaras?

Can Ponies Take Penalties?

Are All Brothers Foul?

Is An Own Goal Bad?

Who Ate All The Pies?

What's Ukrainian For Football?

Who Ate All The Pies?

Helena Pielichaty

WALKER
BOOKS

For Andy Booth, Huddersfield Town legend

First published 2009 by Walker Books Ltd
87 Vauxhall Walk, London SE11 5HJ

10 9 8 7 6 5 4 3 2 1

Text © 2009 Helena Pielichaty
Cover illustration © 2009 Sonia Leong

This book has been typeset in Helvetica and Handwriter

Printed and bound in Great Britain by Clays Ltd, St Ives plc

British Library Cataloguing in Publication Data:
a catalogue record for this book is available from the British Library

ISBN 978-1-4063-1737-4

www.walker.co.uk

☆ ☆ The Team ☆ ☆

☆ **Megan "Meggo" Fawcett** GOAL

☆ **Petra "Wardy" Ward** DEFENCE

☆ **Lucy "Goose" Skidmore** DEFENCE

☆ **Dylan "Dyl" or "Psycho 1" McNeil** LEFT WING

☆ **Holly "Hols" or "Wonder" Woolcock** DEFENCE

☆ **Veronika "Nika" Kozak** MIDFIELD

☆ **Jenny-Jane "JJ" or "Hoggy" Bayliss** MIDFIELD

☆ **Gemma "Hursty" or "Mod" Hurst** MIDFIELD

☆ **Eve "Akka" Akboh** STRIKER

☆ **Tabinda "Tabby" or "Tabs" Shah** STRIKER/MIDFIELD

☆ **Daisy "Dayz" or "Psycho 2" McNeil** RIGHT WING

☆ **Amy "Minto" or "Lil Posh" Minter** VARIOUS

Official name: Parrs Under 11s, also known as the Parsnips

Ground: Lornton FC, Low Road, Lornton

Capacity: 500

Affiliated to: the Nettie Honeyball Women's League
junior division

Sponsors: Sweet Peas Garden Centre, Mowborough

Club colours: red and white; red shirts with white sleeves,
white shorts, red socks with white trim

Coach: Hannah Preston

Assistant coach: Katie Regan

☆ ☆ Star Player ☆ ☆

☆ **Age:** 10

☆ **Birthday:** 29 January

☆ **School:** Saddlebridge C of E Primary

☆ **Position in team:** defence

☆ **Likes:** football, watching Leicester City (the Foxes) with my dad

☆ **Dislikes:** feeling left out sometimes when we train, because I'm the only one in the Parrs Under 11s who goes to my school and everyone else seems to know each other

☆ **Supports:** Leicester City and Leicester City Women's

☆ **Favourite player(s) on team:** Gemma is so talented and Megan is a great goalie and Lucy is good in defence with me

Holly "Wonder" Woolcock

☆ **Best football moment:** when Hannah gave me the nickname Wonderwall because she said the opposition found it so hard to get past me.

☆ **Match preparation:** I make sure I warm up properly.

☆ **Have you got a lucky mascot or a ritual you have to do before or after a match?** I like a hug from my dad.

☆ **What do you do in your spare time?** Follow the Foxes.

☆ **Favourite book(s):** anything by Roald Dahl

☆ **Favourite band(s):** Westlife (or any boy bands)

☆ **Favourite film(s):** Happy Feet

☆ **Favourite TV programme(s):** Blue Peter

Hello! My name is Holly Woolcock and I'm a defender for the Parrs Under 11s. When I begin my part it's almost the end of our first season with only two matches remaining. We're mid-table, which isn't bad, though Dad reckons we could be higher if we fielded our strongest side every time instead of all this "anyone-who-turns-up-gets-a-go malarkey" as he calls it. As you'll find out, my dad can be quite opinionated when it comes to football.

There's going to be a presentation evening after the last match of the season. Most football clubs have a presentation evening, when players are rewarded for their contributions to the team for that season, and the Parrs senior team included us in theirs. We all thought this was so cool, being invited along and treated the same as them. Even the categories for the awards were the same.

So here goes. Just sit down, relax and read on...

Love,
Holly xxx

P.S. I've included the league table as it stands at the beginning of my bit (see next page).

The Nettie Honeyball Women's Football League junior division

Team	P	W	D	L	Pts
Grove Belles	16	14	1	1	43
Tembridge Vixens	16	10	1	5	31
Misslecott Goldstars	16	9	3	4	30
Greenbow United Girls	16	9	2	5	29
Furnston Diamonds	16	9	2	5	29
Parrs U11s	16	8	1	7	25
Cuddlethorpe Tigers	16	5	2	9	17
Hixton Lees Juniors	16	2	7	7	13
Lutton Ash Angels	16	2	1	13	7
Southfields Athletic	16	1	2	13	5

1

We had just finished the six-a-side match at the end of training when Hannah, our coach, asked us to gather round. "Right, gang, we're now going to do something so totally crazy and awesome you won't stop talking about it for weeks," she announced.

We waited. Long seconds passed and the tension became too much for Dylan, who grabbed hold of Daisy, her twin. "What?" Dylan asked. "What?"

"I thought we could…" Hannah began, then paused again.

"What?" Dylan repeated. *"What?"*

"… warm down!"

Everyone groaned and Dylan smacked her forehead in disappointment. "That's not crazy or awesome! That's what we always do!"

"Got your attention, though, didn't I?" Hannah grinned. "OK, girls, spread out along the touchline."

I pushed my sticky fringe off my face and sighed. I didn't need to warm down. I was already warm. In fact, I was boiling hot. And exhausted. And starving hungry.

"OK, one lot of high-step skips forward, then one backwards," Hannah ordered. "Nice and steady and controlled…"

I tried, I really did. I kept my head straight and my eyes forward, but the far side of the pitch seemed miles away. I hadn't even a smidgen of energy left, and the others soon pulled ahead.

Hannah noticed and fell back in step with me. "Come on, Hols! You can do it. Warming down's really important for your muscles."

"I know!" I mumbled.

"Keep your knees high, to get the full range of movement in your hips."

"Mm."

"Like this," she said and demonstrated.

I nodded and swallowed hard, wishing she'd pick on the others instead, the ones without the tummy that bulged over their waistbands when they doubled over.

"OK?" Hannah said.

Taking a deep breath I summoned a pea-sized portion of will-power from somewhere.

"That's more like it!" Hannah complimented as we reached the touchline together. "And back!"

I high-skipped backwards, faster this time to get it over and done with, and I ended up back at the start at the same time as everyone else, but my heart was racing like mad and I knew my face would be redder than a pillar box.

"Carioca!" Katie, our assistant coach, then called from the other end of the line.

Carioca? Phew! This one was just funny walking, like apes trying not to step in a cowpat. I managed that one without bursting any major organs.

"Last one now! Small skips!" Hannah directed.

Even better. Small skips were easy. My heart

managed to slow down to a gallop, and Hannah grinned and put her thumb up to show she was pleased with me.

"Brilliant work, everyone!" she said as we gathered by the touchline. "Help collect all the stuff, then meet back in the changing rooms."

By the time we had cleared away, my breathing had returned to normal and I felt warm instead of hot. I was still *sooooooo* hungry, though! I tried not to think about the Galaxy bar tucked in my bag – my treat ready for when we had finished. I was tempted to open it as we crossed the field, but nobody else was eating and I wasn't going to be the only one. They'd probably think I was being a greedy-guts, especially as I was already the tubbiest on the team.

In the changing rooms, Hannah began giving out sheets of paper. I perched on the edge of the bench next to Lucy and Nika.

"Won't keep you a tick; I just want to go through

some stuff before you all shoot off," Hannah began. "First of all, I presume you're all available for Saturday against Lutton Ash Angels?"

"As long as they're not as dirty as last time," Megan declared. "Otherwise, no."

Everyone knew this was a fib. Megan would turn up whoever the opposition was – angels … werewolves … vampires. "Don't worry," Hannah told her; "I've asked one of our officials from the senior league to ref this one. They won't mess with Bev Bywater."

"Nobody messes with Bev Bywater," Katie added.

"Good," Megan said, as if that settled it.

"Right, these letters are about the presentation evening," Hannah continued.

"I thought you'd given us those last week," Lucy said. She glanced at me as if to say "She did, didn't she?" and I nodded. Saturday 3 May from seven o'clock onwards. There'd be speeches followed by a buffet and a disco. Venue: the function room above the clubhouse. Not that I'd be going, but I'd remembered because it was the day of the last match of the season.

"Hang on, Miss Impatient," Hannah told Lucy. "That letter home was just the basics. This chap is the nitty-gritty. As you'll see when you read it out loud."

"Me? Do I have to?"

"Yep … but I know you're a Man U supporter so just shout if you get stuck on any long words!"

"Cheek!" Lucy squawked and stood up.

I budged up closer to Nika. She's pretty good at speaking English, but I know she finds understanding written information hard sometimes.

"'Girls,'" Lucy began, putting on a fake posh voice, "'it is now time to vote for whoever you think is our player of the season…'" Lucy stopped. "Oh!" she said as the words sank in.

"Yes." Hannah laughed. "'Oh.' That's what we do at presentation evenings. We give out awards. As you were, Skidmore."

"'Your vote for the Players' Player should be for the player you think has given most to the team this season. The player we would miss most if they weren't able to play. You might think that skill or bravery or turning up each week is most important – that's for you to decide. Everyone nominates a first, second and third choice.'"

Hannah's eyes roved round the room. "The one thing I *don't* want you to do is vote for your best friend…"

She paused to let that sink in, but there was no need as far as I was concerned. My best friend was called Lauren O'Brien and she'd rather saw both her legs off than play football.

"… so if I were you I'd keep your vote a secret. Then nobody's going to be worried about offending anyone."

"I am not highly good at keeping secrets." Dylan sighed.

"Try really hard." Hannah smiled.

I turned to Nika. "Did you get all that?" I asked her.

"Yes." She nodded, flashing me a grin. "Best players – one-two-three."

Hannah checked her watch, then clapped her hands together. "All right, gang, buzz off home. The senior team will be arriving any sec. You don't want them trampling over your feet. I need your votes in by next Tuesday at training. OK?"

"OK," we chorused.

2

**Dad was waiting in the car park, and
I sighed with relief.** If it had been Tracie, my
stepmum, it would have taken ages to escape.
She's a lunchtime supervisor at Mowborough
Primary, where three-quarters of the team go,
and they swarm round her like she's some sort of
celebrity who's turned up for a film première. "Hi,
Mrs Woolcock!" "Loving that top, Mrs Woolcock!"
"Did Aisha find her swimming stuff in the end,
Mrs Woolcock?" It's not that I'm jealous – truly
I'm not – it's just that after training all I want to do
is get in the car and eat chocolate.

With Dad, I could do just that.

"Good practice?" he asked, switching on
the engine as I snuggled down in the passenger
seat and burrowed in my bag for the Galaxy.

Just touching it made my stomach leap with joy.
Mmm. Yummy, creamy chocolate. I tore away the
foil wrapper and took a huge bite. "Yeah. Really
good," I mumbled.

"I suppose you spent all your time SAQ-ing."

I nodded. In case you don't know, SAQ stands
for speed, ability and quickness training. It involves
exercises, drills and circuits to make us faster
and more co-ordinated. We do spend most of our
practice time on them, but Dad is not a big fan.

"SAQ! You ought to be playing proper matches,
never mind S-A-bloomin'-Q-ing," he muttered,
his face reddening as he yanked his seatbelt
downwards. I know I've got puppy fat, but my dad's
tummy is well massive. It always takes him at least
three attempts to get the strap over and in.

"Well done!" I said as it finally clicked into place.

He grunted, then spied my Galaxy. "Ooh, let's
have a bite!"

I knew all too well what would happen if I did.
I'd be staring at an empty wrapper and two crumbs

if I was lucky. Maybe even a blood-filled stump where I'd once had a finger! Instead I broke off a square and passed it across to him.

"Sure you can spare it?" he complained.

"I'm starving," I said. "I haven't eaten since lunch."

"Why haven't you eaten? Tracie said she'd made a lovely salad for us. You could have had that before you came out."

"I know," I admitted; "but I can't eat before training. Everyone knows you can't train on a full stomach."

"A bit of salad wouldn't fill you," he said, and slowly reversed out of the car park.

We drove out of Lornton and headed along the Mowborough Road. We then had to go through the town centre and out again to Saddlebridge, the village where we live. It usually takes about half an hour, and in that time we catch up on each other's news. When I say *news*, I mean *football* news, our favourite subject.

As we approached the outskirts of Mowborough,

I mentioned the voting sheet Hannah had given us for Players' Player.

"Oh, well, you know who'll get that, don't you," he said instantly.

"Who?"

"Hursty."

"Why? Why not Megan? She started the team. Or Lucy. Lucy's really strong at the back."

"Hmm. Goose is all right and Meggo's decent enough in goal, but it's Hursty that's got the edge – that innate talent," Dad said.

I grinned. I loved the way Dad took our discussions seriously, using the same phrases he'd use for Leicester City, the team we both support. And he always referred to us by our nicknames. He never called Lucy "Lucy", only "Goose". In fact, I think he was the only one who called her that!

"You can see it a mile off," he continued. "Cracking little player, she is."

"Thanks for not thinking *I* might get it, by the way, Dad," I said, licking my finger and dipping it into the empty Galaxy wrapper in case there were any stray flakes of chocolate still lurking about. "I mean, I'm only your precious daughter."

"You *are* my precious daughter, but it's always the forwards who get the glory, Princess. Check out FIFA's Players of the Year from the past."

"Such as?"

"Ronaldo, Zidane, Ronaldinho, Shevchenko…"

"What about in women's?" I challenged.

"Prinz, Hamm, Marta … the same. All forwards."

I nodded. My dad knows so much. "And then there's the other reason I won't get it," I told him.

"What's that?"

I patted my tummy and grinned. "Fat kids don't win sports trophies!"

He winced. "Don't call yourself that, love."

"Why not? It's true!"

"You're not fat. You've got big bones, like me."

"Big bones covered in chocolate!" I said, and we both laughed.

☆ ☆ ☆

As we neared the market square, Dad pulled the visor down and squinted into the watery evening sun. "I'm just thinking…"

"Uh-huh."

"Tracie's out tonight..."

"Uh-huh."

"So do you fancy a Chinese?"

"From the Lucky Dragon?"

"Where else?"

"And can I have sweet-and-sour chicken with special fried rice and those sesame triangle things?"

"Course. Just don't tell Tracie, eh? If she asks, that salad she left for us was delicious."

"And scrumptious."

"And so tasty."

"Award-winning, in fact."

Twenty minutes later we took our two carrier bags full of foil cartons across to the small play area opposite. We sat on a bench, munching away. Chocolate and Chinese in one night. Bliss!

3

Next morning I was up by half-past six. Not because I wanted to be, but because the birds in the wild cherry tree outside my bedroom window were making such a racket. Springtime's well annoying.

I washed and dressed as quietly as I could and tiptoed downstairs. The kitchen was empty. A side plate speckled with toast crumbs and a half-finished pot of cold tea on the table told me that Dad had already left for work. I knew Tracie wasn't up yet, which meant I could start thinking about who to choose as my Players' Player of the Season.

Deep down I agreed with Dad: Gemma probably would get the award – but that didn't mean I was just going to stick any old names down. You need to think through decisions like this. Mull over them properly. I found the sheet of paper Hannah had given us, then grabbed the notebook from next to the phone and strode into the kitchen.

"Right," I whispered, drawing rough lines down the notebook. "What was it we had to look for?" Skill. Bravery. Turning up. The one you would miss most and the one who has given most. OK, that meant five columns. Six, if you counted one for names.

Name	Who shows most skill?	Who is bravest?	Who would I miss most?	Who turns up on time?	Who has given most?
Megan					

I'd give each player a mark out of ten per column, I decided; then whoever got the most marks altogether would get my first vote, second would get second place and third would get third place. Sorted.

I'd just started to write all the names down the left-hand side when I heard creaking footsteps above me. Tracie was up. Hurriedly I tore the sheet off the notebook, folded it in half and slid it and the letter between the table-mats. Keep it secret, Hannah had said. That meant from everybody.

I walked over to my schoolbag and searched for my lunchbox. I'd just emptied the balled-up clingfilm and squished carton of apple juice into the bin when Tracie came in. "Morning," I said.

"Morning, Holly" – she yawned – "I thought I heard you. Couldn't you sleep?"

"The birds again."

"Ah!" She reached across me and switched on the kettle, her bony wrist jutting out from her dressing gown. Tracie does not have big bones like Dad and me but she is *bony*. She has bony wrists. Bony elbows. Bony cheeks. Bony-bones. "We'll have to get you some earplugs," she said.

"Yeah."

"And at least you see more of the day, being up early."

"That's true."

I ought to have warned you that Tracie and me always have conversations like this. Polite but boring.

While Tracie made herself an instant coffee, I began piling stuff onto the worktop for my lunchbox. Smoky-bacon crisps, two chocolate bars (one for break, one for lunch), then cheese, pickle and bread for my sandwich stuff.

"I can do that for you, Holly," Tracie said. "You get some breakfast."

I took a deep breath. I've been making my own pack-up for school since I was six. I know what I'm doing. "That's OK. I don't mind."

"There's plenty of fruit in the bowl," she said.

Fruit? As if! "I know," I said. "Thanks."

I began with the cheese, trying to cut the orange block of Red Leicester in straight, neat slices. I could feel Tracie staring. After what seemed like a lifetime she went, "I was wondering…" – then stopped.

That made me lose concentration, and my last slice of cheese had a fat wedge at the bottom. To level it out, I spread extra pickle on the thinner end.

"You were wondering?" I prompted, ducking down into the fridge to find a tub of Petits Filous and a chilled carton of blackcurrant juice.

"Are you still set against going to the presentation evening?"

"Uh-huh."

"But from what everyone tells me, it's going to be so much fun."

"Yes, well, I … I just don't fancy it."

"No?"

"No."

"Can you tell me why?"

I shook my head and squashed the lid down on my sandwich box. "Better go and clean my teeth," I said and left her to her coffee.

Later, as I walked to school with Lauren, I thought about Tracie's question. Could I tell her why I didn't want to go? Not really. How would anyone so slim understand how it feels to be the biggest in a group? To stand out like an elephant in a field full of gazelles? Especially when there would be a disco afterwards with everyone dressed up in sparkly, clingy party clothes. No way. It'd be just like when I was a bridesmaid at Dad and Tracie's wedding.

I'd had to wear this horrible pink dress with a tight-fitting bodice and floaty skirt. Just squeezing into it had been an achievement, and when the DJ's lights bounced over me I felt like a sweaty iced doughnut. I still have nightmares about it. After that, I promised myself I would never, ever go to a disco again.

Lauren brought me back to the present by waving her hand in front of my face. "Hello, calling Holly Woolcock, come in, please..."

I shivered. "Sorry. Miles away."

"As usual! I was asking what you think."

"About what?"

"About whether Mr Addy is going out with Miss Camara."

Mr Addy is our form teacher and Miss Camara is our classroom assistant. "The amount of time they spend in the library corner?" I grinned. "Definitely."

4

The rest of the week was the same as ever. I got up, went to school, hung out with Lauren, came home, had a chat with Tracie, watched TV until Dad came back, ate and had a chat with him, went to bed.

I hadn't voted for my Players' Player yet. I had got as far as making a neat copy of my points table on my computer, but I hadn't filled it in. I'm always like this with big decisions; I take for ever to make my mind up. Lauren gets really mad with me sometimes if we're doing group work. "Just say yes or no!" she'll yell at me.

What I did decide was that I'd suss everyone out at the Lutton Ash match. Watch them closely. See how they performed and then grade them. Like sports journalists did in the Sunday papers.

Saturday morning was freezing and windy. I doubled up on my outerwear, especially as Dad and I were going to watch Leicester City against Colchester straight after the Lutton match.

"Make sure you keep warm," Tracie said, wrapping her cardigan round herself as she stood in the doorway.

"You should come with us. It'll blow the cobwebs off you!" Dad told her.

My heart began to pound. Football was *our* thing, not Tracie's. Please say no, I willed her.

As if reading my mind, she glanced at me, then shook her head at Dad. "In this weather? No, thanks!"

"Aw! See you about sixish, then."

"Fine. And remember what I told you," she called after him.

"Yeah, yeah," Dad said dismissively and hurried to the car.

"What do you have to remember that she told you?" I asked as he started the engine.

"What? Oh, nothing important."

☆ ☆ ☆

We arrived at the ground half an hour before
kick-off. Even after I'd jogged round the field and
we'd had a short pre-match shooting practice,
I still didn't want to strip off. I gave Dad my stuff
to carry just seconds before the match started.

"Eh, Hol" – he grinned – "look at the ref; she'd
terrify Robbie Savage, she would."

I turned round. This I had to see! The Bev that
Hannah had told us about was chatting to Hannah,
Katie and the Lutton Ash coach. She was shorter
than all of them, but had much broader shoulders and
solid calves that bulged beneath her black socks like
turnips. As she nodded at something Hannah said,
I could tell there was a no-nonsense air about her.
I smiled. The Angels wouldn't get away with a thing
today, and that meant I could concentrate on grading
my team-mates on skill, bravery and the rest.

I gave Dad a quick cuddle, then went to stand
with the gang.

We huddled together and waited for Hannah's

pep talk – but every time she tried to speak, her hair whipped across her face and she kept having to spit it out of her mouth. "Pht! Puh! Pah! OK, girls. As you can see, it's really windy today. So what do we need to do?"

"Wear an ultra-protective moisturizer," Amy stated as she smoothed on her lip-gloss.

I was the only one who giggled. Amy cracks me up with her comments, but everyone else takes her far too seriously. They don't realize that half the time she's only winding them up.

"Anything else?" Hannah asked. "With the ball?"

"Keep it low," Lucy said.

That was a point in her Players' Player column from me right there. For knowledge. Except there wasn't a knowledge column. Maybe there should be one? Oh, heck!

"Nice one! Keep it low or it's going to end up going all over the place, except where you want it to go, so be aware of the ball and be aware of one another."

"Be aware of that number 5!" Megan added and everyone laughed. Number 5 had been the nastiest of the bunch last time.

Bev held her arm up to show she was ready if we were. I twisted from side to side, raring to go. I loved this moment just before the whistle blew, with the whole match ahead of us. I loved it when I was watching City and I loved it when I was playing. I loved it because once that whistle went, anything could happen. That was what made football brilliant.

We had lost the toss earlier, so we were playing into the wind. Gemma kicked off, passing back to Nika, who dribbled forward – but she was already struggling, fighting to keep the ball at her feet and stay upright at the same time. All the Angels had remained in their half and, as Nika prepared to pass, three of them crowded round her. She looked up, saw there was nowhere to go and back-heeled the ball. Good tactic. Worth a point from me. Unfortunately there was no one behind her to receive it and it rolled out for a Lutton throw-in.

"One of you!" their coach bellowed from the touchline. "Shell! Look sharp!"

My heart leapt. Action stations! I ran forward to the edge of the box, ready to defend once the throw had been taken. And guess who Shell was? Little old number 5.

At least she can't foul anyone taking a throw-in, I thought, watching as she grabbed the ball. Well, I was right, she didn't foul. In fact, what happened next was really funny. When she went to throw the ball in, her arms flew forwards but the ball flew backwards! The wind must have caught it. Everyone laughed, including the ref – but not in a nasty way. It just looked amusing.

"Take it again." Bev smiled.

Shell looked grim and determined this time – but exactly the same thing happened; just as one of the Angels got free and she aimed, the wind had other ideas and carried the ball backwards.

"And again!" Bev called.

Shell shook her head. "*You* do it," she snarled at one of her team-mates, kicking the ball at her in a temper. As the replacement Angel took up position, Shell backed towards me. Glancing over her shoulder to make sure there was nobody behind her, she caught me still grinning. Her eyes narrowed darkly. "What are *you* laughing at?" she asked.

"Nothing. It just looked funny," I told her.

"Not as funny as you do, fatso," she growled.

A lump came to my throat. Nobody had ever called me names on the pitch before. At school a few times, but never at football. I felt my stomach clench but I didn't say anything. I'm not very good at comebacks. The throw-in had been taken and I concentrated on that instead.

For the next fifteen to twenty minutes we dominated, and play rarely came anywhere near Megan, Lucy and me at the back. Lucy moved up to midfield to assist from there, but the wind was definitely on Lutton's side and every attempt we had saw the ball whipped wider, higher or further than intended. "We can't *buy* a goal today," Megan said, banging her hands together to keep warm.

"I know," I said, on red alert as one of the Angels almost careered into Dylan – before checking herself as Bev came into her eyeline. "It's not fair."

"And boring! I hate matches like this when there's nothing to do. I wish I'd brought something to read!" Megan spoke too soon. A defending Angel in the right-hand channel found herself with the ball at her feet and whacked it as hard and low as she could. It scythed through the grass and found their horrible number 5 just inside our half. She stopped the ball with her boot, turned, then dribbled it forward, the Lutton Ash spectators roaring her on. "Go on, Shell!" "Have a shot!" "Finish it! Finish it!"

My heart was thumping. No way was she going to finish it! Not after what she'd called me. Usually Lucy's the speedy one, but I sprinted as fast as a deer to intercept that ball. Shell looked up, saw me coming and hesitated. Instead of shooting there and then she attempted to kick the ball forward, hoping to run onto it. Nuh-uh – not happening. I had closed her right down by then and simply stuck my leg out to deflect the ball behind for Megan to clear.

Then something weird happened. Shell threw herself on the ground, right where my foot had been, and started rolling around, clutching her shin in agony. "Ow! Ow! That kills!" she cried. "She did a sliding tackle on me! They're well dangerous! Ow! Ow! Ow!"

"Ref*ere*e!" voices from the touchline bellowed.

I had my hands on my knees, puffed out from the run. When I glanced up I saw two angry faces, a man and a woman; they were pacing up and down and pointing at me. "Dangerous play, referee!" the man called.

"Ow! Ow! Ow!" Shell continued.

By now a couple more of the Angels had gathered round the writhing player, bending over her like she'd been shot or something, and I was beginning to feel worried. What if she wasn't faking? Maybe I had caught her shin by accident... I didn't think

I had, but I'd been so focused on getting to the ball I might have done. What if I'd broken a bone or something?

A stern voice behind me soon cleared up that idea. "No foul. Free kick to the Parrs," Bev said briskly, nodding at me.

"What?" the woman from the touchline shouted in disbelief. "*What?* Are you blind, referee?"

Bev's head snapped round and I swear I saw her nostrils flare. "'Scuse me?" she asked.

"I said, are you blind? That's my daughter down there injured."

"In case you hadn't noticed," the man added.

"Injured? The only thing that's injured is her ego. Now I suggest you keep your opinions to yourselves, or I'll have you and all your supporters ten yards back for the rest of the match. Is that clear?" Her words came out like ice cubes. Freezing cold and definitely clear.

The woman scowled and the man opened his mouth, but he closed it when Shell jumped up and started chasing the ball again – though not before she had mouthed "whale meat" at me. I was really beginning to dislike that girl.

Lucy, the twins and I were rested for the start of the second half. I was glad, as it gave me a chance to watch my team-mates in action and because I was feeling tired and hungry. I hadn't eaten breakfast and my stomach was beginning to rumble.

We began strongly. With the wind in our direction we played as if we had wings, and our forwards bombarded the Lutton Ash end. It wasn't long before we scored twice in quick succession, with a third goal minutes later from Jenny-Jane.

After JJ had scored, Shell and the number 8 seemed to target her, often backing into her accidentally-on-purpose when she wasn't even near play. Even Bev missed some of their sly digs.

"Unbelievable!" Hannah kept saying, pacing up and down and signalling a rolling motion across to Katie. "Absolutely unbelievable. Holly, are you ready to go back on? I think your stable presence is called for. JJ will end up lamping one of them otherwise."

"OK," I said and began stretching my calf muscles.

The first thing Shell did when she saw me coming back on was sneer. "Here she comes. Wobble, wobble, wobble. No need to ask who ate all the pies!"

I ignored her. If Jenny-Jane Bayliss could keep her temper, just about, then so could I, just about. Instead, I replied by blocking every single ball that came her way.

We won five–nil in the end. I wished it had been fifty.

5

There isn't enough time on Saturdays between the end of my match and the beginning of City's match to go home.

Instead Dad and I head straight for Gilbert Way, with me pulling my City top on over my Parrs top and my tracky bottoms over my shorts, and swapping my boots for trainers while he drives.

Now that the tension of the Lutton Ash match was over, my tummy was going, "Hello! Remember me?"

"Dad, I'm famished! Can we have …" I almost said "a pie", but stopped. Stupid Smelly Shell.

"… fish and chips when we get there?"

He hesitated. "I dunno, Hol…"

I couldn't understand why he was being so reluctant. "And mushy peas. It'd be rude not to have mushy peas!" I needed food. Lots of it. To fill my empty tummy and to fill that other empty hole which seemed deeper after the name-calling.

"I was thinking we could call in at a cafe or something … for a change," Dad mumbled.

"Aw, why? Fish and chips, please! It's what we do! And I'm starving."

"I know, but…"

"Mouth-watering succulent crispy fried fish…" I am really good at adjectives and went on and on – "… delicious golden brown chunky home-made chips …" – until Dad shook his head in submission and laughed.

"OK, OK, you win; you've convinced me."

So we walked along Aylestone Road towards Gilbert Way, taking huge bites of fish and dipping hot, tasty chips into our peas one at a time. Mega-tasty! In the ground afterwards I talked Dad into buying us a bag of chocolate éclairs from the refreshment kiosk. You have to have something to chew at half-time as well as your fingernails, you know! It's the law.

Hey, remember I was saying anything could happen in football? Well, we were one–nil down when Iain Hume came on as a sub and scored in the eighty-ninth minute. Yes! We chanted, "Ee-aye-ee-aye-ee-aye-oh, up the football league we go!" in the car all the way home.

Tracie was just as happy as we were when we returned. Her face shone when Dad greeted her with a huge peck on the forehead.

"How's my adorable wife?" he asked her.

"All the better for seeing you both." She turned to me. "I heard the City score on the radio. What about you? Did you win?"

"Five–nil!"

Tracie pretended to look astonished. "Five–nil! Brilliant!"

"Hols played a blinder," Dad added.

"As she always does!"

Not true, but I let it pass.

"So what have you been up to?" Dad asked her.

"I've been experimenting with Gordon Ramsay."

"Have you now? Where is he? I'll kill him!" Dad joked, pretending to search under the table.

I laughed, happy to hand him over to Tracie. "I'll leave you lovebirds alone," I told them, planning to fill in my Players' Player form while the morning match was still buzzing in my head. "See you later."

"Don't be long. Dinner'll be ready in five minutes," Tracie trilled, swatting Dad's hand as he patted her bottom.

Five minutes? I was still stuffed from lunch; no way could I eat in five minutes. I pulled an apologetic face, quickly wiping my mouth with the back of my hand in case I had any chocolate round it. "Eek! Sorry, Tracie, but I'm really full from the fish and chips. Is it OK if I have mine a bit later on?"

"Well…" She frowned at Dad, then glanced towards the hob where various pans were boiling away. "I suppose so."

"Cheers!" I bolted upstairs and switched on my computer. Time to get down to business.

6

I printed off the empty table and pencilled in my scores. In the end it didn't take that long. I think it actually helped that I didn't know any of my team-mates from school or anything, because I didn't feel I had to give more marks to people just because they were in my class. I bet some of them were in a real tangle over who to vote for – Megan, for one. Petra was her best friend but she was only so-so as a player. Megan couldn't honestly vote for her.

In the end Megan, Lucy and Gemma were my top three, with Megan just pipping Lucy to the top. I was glad Amy would never see my sheet. If I could have given her marks for being the prettiest or having the best accessories she'd have won by a mile, but as it was meant to be about actual skill…

Anyway, this was how my final scores looked:

My Players' Player of the Season

Name	Who shows most skill?	Who is bravest?	Who would I miss most?	Who turns up on time?	Who has given most?	Total
Megan	8	10	9	10	10	47
Lucy	9	9	9	9	9	45
Gemma	10	9	8	8	8	43
Jenny-Jane	6	10	10	7	9	42
Nika	8	8	8	7	8	39
Eve	7	8	8	7	7	37
Tabinda	6	6	9	7	8	36
Petra	5	5	9	7	8	34
Daisy	6	7	4	7	6	30
Dylan	5	7	4	7	6	29
Amy	1	0	7	8	2	18

I trundled downstairs, feeling pleased with myself.
I wanted to show my scoring system to Dad, and
I wouldn't mind Tracie having a peep, too – as long
as she promised not to tell her fan club!

☆ ☆ ☆

My hand was on the kitchen-door handle when I stopped. I could hear Dad and Tracie on the other side, their voices raised. "What else could I do?" Dad was saying. "It's what we've always done, since she was little. It's tradition."

I frowned. Were they talking about me?

"But it's got to stop! You know it has!" Tracie said.

"Oh, lighten up, love! One lot of fish and chips isn't the end of the world."

"And what else?"

"A few chocolate éclairs."

"Andy!"

"What?"

"Do you know the fat content of fish and chips and 'a few' chocolate éclairs?" Her voice had a cold edge to it I'd never heard before.

"Oh, come on, Tracie, for Pete's sake. One step at a time, eh?"

"You haven't said anything to her, have you?" Tracie asked.

"I didn't want to upset her."

"But you promised! You know talking about food is better coming from you than me."

"I know, but…"

"She never listens to me. I suggested she take some fruit to school the other day and you'd think I'd asked her to jump off a cliff!"

My heart was thudding in my chest. I felt sick. So that's what this was all about – she was putting me on a diet! Putting me on a diet so I would be as bony as her. Well, I didn't want to be as bony as her. I wanted to be round and cuddly like my dad. No matter what *she* thought, or what stupid names stupid people like Smelly Shell called me.

There was a long silence on the other side of the door. Then Tracie mumbled something I couldn't hear and Dad said in a low voice that he'd wash up, and Tracie told him not to bother – she needed something to do.

I agreed with Tracie totally; she *did* need something to do. Like butting out of my business for a start. I turned and headed back upstairs.

7

I kept out of Tracie's way as much as I could for the rest of the weekend. Most of the time I stayed in my room or hid behind a book. On Sunday evening I made my packed lunch for Monday so I could avoid her at breakfast.

I felt churned up inside. So that was how she'd felt about me all along. She thought I ate too much. She thought I was a blob. She was just as bad as Shell – except at least Shell called me names to my face. This was worse. Shell was the opposition. Tracie was meant to be on my side.

I couldn't even complain to Dad about it; there was no point. He'd only go all pathetic and say he didn't want to take sides. It was at times like this when I wished I had brothers or sisters to turn to, but I didn't. Instead I had Lauren.

☆ ☆ ☆

On Monday morning we were sitting under the willow arch at break, and Lauren listened while I ranted on about Tracie.

"It's begun, then," she said.

"What has?"

Lauren plucked at something stuck to her sweatshirt. "She's starting to take over."

"Is she?"

"Yup. She wants your dad to herself, see."

I felt my skin tingle all over. That was my worst nightmare: Mum left when I was just a baby because she wasn't cut out for "the stress of family life" – and now Dad was getting taken away.

"'Fraid so," Lauren continued. "It happened to my cousins when my Uncle Liam remarried. You watch. At first they're all lovey-dovey and sucking up to you – Tracie's done that bit, hasn't she?"

"She has been pretty kind, so far," I admitted.

"Mmm. Well, that's step one – then step two starts."

"Step two?"

"Step two's where they start criticizing and trying to dictate the little things, right, like what food you can eat and what clothes you can wear and that..."

"Uh-huh."

"After that is step three. You don't want to get to step three."

"Why? What's step three?" I could hardly breathe.

Lauren looked at me from behind the special blue glasses she wore for her dyslexia. "Boarding school."

"Boarding school?"

"That's what happened to my cousins."

"Really?"

"Really. And you don't want to go to boarding school. It's nothing like Hogwarts."

"No?"

"There's no Sorting Hat. Nothing."

"Right."

"Watch out for the little things, Hol. That's my tip."

"I will," I said. "I will."

I knew Dad and Tracie would never send me to boarding school – we didn't have enough money, for a start. I was less sure about the little things, though. I would definitely be watching out for the little things.

8

The first little thing came before training the very next day. "I'll pick you up, Holly," Tracie said as she dropped me off at the ground. "See you out here at half-seven, OK?"

"Why isn't Dad picking me up?" I asked, immediately suspicious. Dad's a lorry driver and I knew he'd only got deliveries in Birmingham and Tamworth that day. No long-distance drops.

"I thought we could have a little chat. Is that OK?"

"What about?" I asked.

She looked uneasy. "I'd prefer to talk about it later."

I scowled. "Well, if this is what I think it's about, you can get lost!" I told her, and slammed the car door hard.

☆ ☆ ☆

I walked briskly across to the practice pitch, feeling so angry. A little chat! You know what you can do with that little chat, Tracie – take it for a little walk over a little cliff!

Hannah was standing by the goalposts, surrounded by the rest of the team. At first I presumed they were all crowding round her to hand in their voting slips, but when I got closer I realized from the buzz of conversation that something else was going on.

"Is it broken?" Petra was asking.

"No, no, just heavily bruised."

"So are you out for the rest of the season?" Jenny-Jane wanted to know.

"Probably, but we've only one match left. It's no biggie."

Nudging my way between Amy and Gemma, I could see that Hannah was on crutches, her left foot heavily bandaged.

She grinned at me. "Hi, Holly. I was just explaining about my ankle. I've sprained it."

"Oh no. How?" I asked.

"I fell awkwardly on it during our match on Sunday. It means I'm not going to be able to train properly with you tonight, and Katie's had to work…"

"So is there no training, then?" I asked, dreading the thought.

"Don't panic! There's training, but not as we know it. I'm just waiting for Bev to arrive."

"Bev the stoppy-starter?" Dylan asked.

"Bev the referee," Hannah corrected, before sending Megan to ask her Auntie Mandy, the clubhouse manager, if it was OK to go up. "We're using the function room tonight," she explained.

Two minutes later there was a whistle from the upstairs window. "Ready when you are!" Megan called.

Upstairs, there was a mad rush as everyone tried to get nearest to Hannah. Dylan and Daisy managed to bag either side of one long crimson seat. They looked like little blonde bookends. I sloped in last, perching on the far end of a corner seat with Lucy and Tabinda.

When we'd all settled, Hannah began. "OK, girls, I'd planned on doing this at the beginning of next season, but now's as good a time as any. We're going to talk about something vital to every footballer…"

"That's easy. A cool haircut," Amy said.

I laughed. Maybe a bit too loudly, but I was grateful to Amy for cheering me up. A cool haircut! Classic Amy!

"Close," Hannah said. "Healthy eating."

I felt as if I'd had a bucket of iced water thrown over me. What? Of all the things I didn't want to talk about! There were groans from loads of the others too, which surprised Hannah as much as me.

"What's wrong?" she asked, her eyes wide.

"We're doing that at school," Tabinda told her; "it's all we hear about from Mr Glasshouse in assembly."

"Food is made up of protein, carbohydrates,

fat, vitamins and minerals," Petra recited.

"Make sure you eat five portions of fruit and veg a day…" Lucy continued.

"Drink plenty of water," Nika chipped in.

"Too much junk food makes your nose drop off," Eve added. We all stared at her. "OK, I made that up."

Ha! So *that* was where Tracie had got the diet idea from. Mowborough Primary. I might have known.

Hannah waggled her bandaged foot. "Well, sorree for wasting your time here, experts. Looks like I asked poor Bev to leave work early for nothing."

"What does she do?" Daisy asked.

"She's a sports nutritionist. One of the best; she works with top athletes and teams to help them plan their diets."

"Wicked job!" Megan said.

"It is," Hannah agreed. "And we'll hear all about it any minute now."

That's when I decided "we" wouldn't include me.

"I need the toilet," I said. "Anyone know where it is?"

"Through there," Megan said, directing me to the other side of the room.

I hurried across the function room, ignoring the wooden dance floor with the glitter ball dangling over it. Glitter ball! There'd been one of those at the wedding. *That* could just drop to the floor and smash into a thousand pieces, for a start!

9

In the Ladies I headed for the end cubicle and sat on the toilet, staring at the door.

It wasn't a very interesting door. Just a plain cream colour with a dull metal lock. I turned and stared at the wall on my right instead. This was only slightly more interesting. The wall was papered with one lot of ghastly floral print separated from another lot of ghastly floral print by one of those wide borders running through the middle. Someone had torn a bit of the border off. Without thinking, I began picking at the loose edge with my nail. This was cool. I could sit here for an hour picking wallpaper, easy.

I'd managed to create a perfect cumulonimbus shape in the border when an unexpected banging on the door made me jump.

"Hols? Are you OK?" Megan asked.

"Yeah, I'm fine."

"Bev's here."

"I'll be out in a bit," I said, but I couldn't keep the quiver out of my voice or the sudden tears from prickling my eyes. I wiped them away hastily. Dumb tears. Where had they come from?

"Hols?"

"Mmm?"

"You sound funny."

"I'm ... er ... not feeling well. Gut rot."

"Oh."

"Don't wait for me. I don't know how long I'll be."

"OK."

I let out a long sigh and waited to hear the outer door bang so I could get back to my paper-picking.

Instead Megan called my name again. "Hols?"

"Yeah?"

"You're not ... um ... hiding, are you?"

"Hiding? Why would I be hiding?" I said. My voice all croaky.

She hesitated. "I just wondered. What with the

session being about eating. I mean, I know you're a bit self-conscious about ... er ... stuff like that."

I jutted out my jaw. No prizes for guessing who'd told her that! "I don't know what you mean," I said. "I'm not self-conscious about anything."

"Everybody's self-conscious about something," Megan said. "I'm self-conscious about my hair. I get called Ginger Nut all the time and it drives me mad. Like, dur – original! I'm thinking of dyeing it black."

I leaned forward and pulled the door open. "But I like your hair. It's a beautiful colour. And so curly."

Megan, leaning with her back against the sink, pulled a face. "It's all right, I suppose. I'd love it to be more like yours, though."

"Mine?"

"More a wee bit wavy than too crazy curly."

"Oh."

"And Eve hates her feet."

"Sorry?"

"Eve hates her feet. Her mum told my mum."

"Her feet?"

"They're a size seven already. She thinks she'll have to wear boats for shoes by the time she starts secondary."

"I've never noticed she's got big feet."

"Exactly. We don't notice each other's faults, do we. Just our own."

"I guess."

Megan glanced towards the outer door, then stepped a little closer. "Look, I heard what that number 5 said on Saturday ... the pie thing..."

I felt myself go hot and cold at the same time. "It's just a football chant. Players get called stuff like that all the time," I blustered.

"I know," Megan said, twisting a friendship bracelet round and round her wrist, "but it's still not nice. I was well angry! I was going to go up to her and say something, but you seemed so calm I thought I'd take your lead and ignore her too – but I felt bad all weekend."

I stared at her. "Why?"

"Why? 'Cos I'm the captain and I should have

stuck up for you." She blinked, and for a second I thought she was going to well up. "I let you down and I'm really sorry."

"It doesn't matter," I mumbled.

"It does. What sort of captain doesn't stick up for her players?"

"You're a great captain," I said. "I'd follow you anywhere."

"In that case," she said softly, "follow me into the function room."

I hesitated. "What if everybody stares?"

"Why would they stare? All they know is I've gone to fetch you from the toilets. They're probably still rearranging the furniture and stuff."

Still I hesitated.

Megan lunged forward and grabbed my arm, pulling me out of the cubicle. "Come on, Woolcock. It's not all about you, you know! This'll be interesting. Trust me."

So I followed her, because you don't disobey your captain.

10

Megan was right. Bev was still unloading folders from a huge briefcase and getting organized, so I knew I hadn't missed anything. Nobody was giving me knowing looks or sidelong glances, but Tabinda gave me a smile and hitched up when I took my place, as if nothing had happened. Megan sat back down with Petra without batting an eyelid. I relaxed. I could do this. I could listen to Bev for an hour and a bit on the subject of healthy eating.

She began by looking round at us all. "Before I start, I want to say I was really impressed with you on Saturday. Not just for being so disciplined against Foulers United – as Lutton Ash *should* be called – but for wanting to play football. Participating in regular exercise is so important at your age. You can't imagine how much your body will thank you for being sporty when you're older, so well done you!"

Everyone sat up that little bit straighter.

Bev lifted a laminated A4 sheet from the table in front of her and held it face down on her lap. "OK, let's kick off. First of all, when I talk about healthy eating, I'm not talking about low-calorie, sugar-free, no-fat, eat-only-boiled-cabbage and other dumb diets. Forget all that…"

Ha! I thought. In your face, Tracie!

"I'm talking about choosing the right things to eat at the right time to fit in with your body's needs that day. For instance, hands up, how many of you don't have breakfast before a match?"

I cheated and kept my hand down because I guessed from Bev's tone that having no breakfast wasn't the right thing to do. Megan, Jenny-Jane and Gemma had theirs in the air, though.

"No good, you guys," Bev said with a shake of her head.

"But I get so nervous," Megan explained.

Bev sighed. "I know. I used to be the same when I played, but you should try to have *something*. It doesn't have to be massive. Beans on toast, Weetabix, just a banana if you can't face much – but if you don't have anything you'll run out of steam halfway through the game. You have to give your body some fuel to run off, just like petrol in a car."

I thought back to my rumbling stomach during the Lutton Ash match and to how tired I'd been at training last week. I could see her point.

"And tell me, afterwards, are you famished?" she asked them.

They all nodded, and Gemma revealed that her mum always told her she needed a trough, not a plate. Gemma Hurst. Our star player ate like a pig!

"That's the trouble," Bev continued. "You get over-hungry. Your body goes into starvation mode and doesn't want you to stop filling."

"Then the petrol spills all down the side of the

car and makes such a mess!" Daisy said.

"Well, in a way," said Bev, nodding, "except the food spills inside the body and your poor old digestive system has to deal with the overload. Speaking of which, have a look at this guy." She held up the sheet from her lap.

It showed a powerfully built swimmer, his arms outstretched as if he'd just won a race, his face lit up in triumph. He had broad, toned shoulders but his waist tapered right in and his stomach was as flat and hard as an iron.

"Introducing Michael Phelps, the American Olympian, also known as the human dolphin. This is what he eats for breakfast when he's training. Here goes ..." – Bev paused for effect, like my teacher does when he reads a really sad bit in *Private Peaceful* out to us in class – "... three fried-egg sandwiches, toast, an omelette, porridge, three pancakes and two cups of coffee."

"That's what I call an overload." Petra gasped.

"I know," Bev agreed, "and I haven't even

mentioned what he has for lunch and dinner. Altogether he consumes twelve thousand calories a day."

"But Mr Glasshouse told us an adult's only supposed to have about two thousand calories," Tabinda said, "and that guy has that for breakfast, just about. He should be massive."

"He should be a whale, not a dolphin," Dylan suggested.

I shifted uncomfortably in my seat, remembering Shell's comment about whales on Saturday. I glanced across at Megan but she was staring at the photograph, absorbed.

Bev shrugged. "He should. Why do you think he isn't?"

Lucy's hand shot up. "He burns it off."

"Give that girl a gold star. Phelps trains six hours a day, six days a week, and swims fifty miles in that week. Fifty miles! That's like swimming the English Channel and back."

"Wow! Respect!" Lucy said.

Bev began delving into her case again. "Obviously Mr Phelps's calorie intake is an extreme example. Us mere mortals can survive on *slightly* less than that…" For a second she stopped foraging and looked up. "By the way, what I don't want is for any of you to get obsessed with the word 'calorie'. A calorie is just the unit used for measuring energy, OK? Like metres and centimetres for length, and seconds and minutes for time. It's not anything to be scared of. Same with the word 'diet' – when I use it, it just means the food we eat and isn't anything to do with losing or gaining weight. OK?"

"OK," we muttered back.

"Good, because say the words 'calorie' and 'diet' to some people – women and teenage girls, especially – and they have a panic attack. If I had my way I'd ban every fashion magazine in the world."

"Not *Sweet Fifteen*! That's my favourite!" Amy protested.

"*Especially Sweet Fifteen*," Bev said firmly.

"Try *Fair Game* instead. You'll be much better off."

"I read that. My mum gets it for her PE department," Lucy said. "It's cool."

As Bev went back to rummaging in her briefcase we began comparing magazines we all read. Amy was still protesting about *Sweet Fifteen,* but Eve made us laugh by saying that *Fireman Sam* was loads better, and Megan was swearing by *The Simpsons*. I caught her eye and grinned, to show her I was OK and that she was right – I *was* finding all this interesting. She grinned back. I was so glad I'd made her my Players' Player of the Season.

Bev now began dealing out laminated A4 sheets, telling us to take two or three each. "These pictures are all of athletes or sportsmen and -women. Their pictures are on the front, their typical diets on the back. Have a look through them and tell me what you notice. Work in small groups if you prefer."

All around me I could hear squeals when someone got a picture of a person they recognized. "Oh!

I've got Rafa Nadal!" "Mine's Kelly Holmes!" "After you with Karen Carney!" "Tom Daly! Tom Daly is *gorgeous*!"

I had Paula Radcliffe, Stevie Gerrard and Barbora Spotakova, a javelin-thrower from the Czech Republic. It was really interesting looking at what they all ate. Grilled fish and chicken seemed most popular – but Paula Radcliffe preferred ostrich meat. Ostrich? Yeuw!

"That'd be like eating a big budgie," Lucy said when I showed her.

"OK," Bev said after a while, "let's talk."

Despite how we had reacted at the beginning, everyone did now seem eager to talk. First up was Amy. I expected her to say something flippant – but she didn't. "I can't get over how different all their body shapes are. I mean, you kind of think of athletes as all looking the same, but they don't, do they."

"Exactly, exactly," Bev said, sounding delighted, as if Amy had hit on some amazing discovery. "Their physiques vary according to their discipline. And because their physiques differ, so do their nutritional needs. A male heavyweight boxer's intake will differ from a female gymnast's, for instance."

"For sure," Amy agreed.

"But what about in football?" Lucy asked.

Bev cocked her head to one side. "What do you mean?"

"Well, I get what you're saying about different shapes for different athletes, but in professional football they're all doing the same thing – but they're still all different builds. You only have to look at them when they're all lined up at the beginning of an international."

"Like Peter Crouch and Shaun Wright-Phillips," Megan added.

"Oh, these two, you mean," Bev said. She whipped out a picture of the two England players standing on the touchline, with Crouchy – or Two-metre Peter as my dad calls him – grinning down at titchy Shaun. "I know what you mean," she told

Lucy, "but in professional football you all have different positions. Each position favours a certain type of frame. Look at all of you, for example..."

Oh no, I thought. Please don't.

11

"There're your small but nippy wingers..."
Bev continued. She nodded to the twins, who
leaned across Hannah and high-fived each other.
"And then there's your solid defender at the back..."
She looked straight at me.

I knew she'd single me out! Knew it! I felt my
cheeks flame with embarrassment. My eyes flew
across to Megan's for help, but she just pointed
to her hair.

"What's your name?" Bev asked me.

"Holly," I mumbled.

"Right, everyone. Why is Holly perfect in
defence?"

Perfect? What was she talking about? I began to
squirm in my seat, while all around me hands shot
up with "ooh-ohh-oh"s coming from all directions.

"Because she doesn't get bundled off the ball."

"She's strong."

"She scares the pants off 'em," Jenny-Jane declared.

"Precisely!" Bev laughed. "In football you need someone strong and more substantially built at the back. That's why that number 5 got so frustrated on Saturday. She couldn't get past Holly so she threw a wobbly. But Holly can also move well. Did any of you see the ground she covered to make the tackle?"

I felt Lucy nudge me on the arm. I nudged her back.

"We did," Hannah said, winking at me; "that's why we love her! She's our little Wonderwall."

Blimey. I never thought I'd get compliments for being the biggest on the team! I went even redder, if that was possible, and I had to focus on the tips of my trainers to get myself together.

"So," Bev said, returning to her point, "athletes can be tall, short, wide or narrow, but the one thing they have in common is that they all need to be *fit*. And choosing the right things to eat is a massive part of that fitness."

She returned to her briefcase and dished out more pictures – this time of meals from around the world. Each picture had a tiny flag in the corner to show its nationality. There were pictures of German sausages with sauerkraut and Polish *bigos* and Italian pizzas and Jamaican jerk chicken. It made my mouth water just looking at them. "Right, choose a country," Bev instructed.

I grabbed the pictures of Chinese food.

"Snap!" Lucy grinned at me as we pounced.

For this task, we had to see which were the healthier choices from each nation by looking at the protein, sugar and fat content of each dish. To help us, there was like a traffic-light spot next to each choice, with red being high in fat or sugar, amber being medium and green being low. I nearly fainted when I saw that battered sweet-and-sour pork (red) had twice as much fat as chop suey (green-amber), and my dad's favourite, spare ribs (red), had *three* times as much. And that was without the fried rice and sesame triangles, which were red as well. Oops!

"So, any thoughts?" Bev asked after we'd all been through several menus.

Gemma put her hand up this time. "I'm really surprised that some meals that I thought were bad for you are not that bad, but some I thought were OK kind of aren't."

"Exactly." Bev nodded. "That's why reading labels is important. Look out for high sugars in carbohydrates especially. They can really catch you out. Or, better still, use only fresh ingredients. Then you know the meal hasn't got any grotty additives chucked in. Any other observations?"

When Eve stuck her hand in the air, I couldn't help glancing down at her feet. They didn't look that big to me, just normal. I glanced away again and listened.

"Yeah. You say all that," Eve said, "but the man I'm going to marry, Usain Bolt, right, trains on chicken nuggets…"

"Uh-huh."

"… and that Phelps dude eats fried-egg sandwiches…"

"Yep."

"That's not exactly what you'd call healthy eating…"

"I agree."

"… but they're both world-record holders."

"And Paula Radcliffe eats chocolate pre-training," I piped up, remembering what else had been on her list apart from the ostrich meat.

"Busted!" Bev laughed. "That's the trouble with role models – they can let you down! OK, let's look at the chocolate issue. Paula, like many long-distance runners, needs the iron and the quick energy boost that chocolate provides."

"So we're allowed chocolate?" Eve asked.

"Of course. If you fancy chocolate, eat chocolate. You'll only crave it more if you don't."

"Good," Eve said, "because chocolate is my life."

Tabinda raised her hand. "So what you're saying

is, we can eat most things but we've got to make sure we exercise too?"

"Got it in one." Bev looked across at Hannah. "Bright girls, these."

Hannah held out her hands. "What can I say? They've learned from the best!"

Bev began collecting in all the pictures and photographs. "Well, I hope you've all got something out of this. I've belted through it, but I've got a website with advice and tips – including healthy recipes – if you want to know more. Hannah will give you the address."

"I will," Hannah said.

"Right, I'd better get going. I've got food plans for a paraplegic archer and two women's cricket teams to complete by tomorrow."

"We really appreciate your time, Bev. You've been awesome. What do we say to Bev, you guys?" Hannah asked us.

"Three cheers!" Megan bellowed, and we all obliged.

"Thanks," Bev said. "Got to dash."

Nika rushed to open the door for her and we all waved goodbye.

Hannah reached for her crutches. "We'd better all scat too before we're booted out."

Everyone began to gather their stuff. I bent down to reach for my bag at the same time as Lucy did for hers, and we almost bumped heads. Seeing her so close reminded me of something. For a second I couldn't remember what, but then it hit me – the voting slips! I pulled mine from the top of my bag, making sure it was folded flat so Lucy couldn't peek, and began waving it in the air. "Hannah! The votes for the Players' Player," I yelled.

Her eyes flew wide. "I'd totally forgotten. Honestly, what am I like? Holly, you're not just Wonder*wall*, you're wonder*brain*, too. You know what? We might as well just call you Wonder and have done!"

12

I clattered down the clubhouse steps but slowed when I reached the bottom, remembering that Tracie was picking me up. We hadn't exactly parted on a high. I took a deep breath. Let's get it over with, I thought – but when I spotted Dad waiting in the car instead of Tracie my heart soared. I pelted towards him. "Hi, Dad!" I said, jumping in on the passenger side. "How's things?"

"So-so."

"Nice day at the office?"

Dad glanced at me, his face long and serious. "Let's cut the small talk."

Uh-oh.

He tugged at his seatbelt in irritation. "Do you need three guesses why I'm here instead of Tracie?"

I didn't reply.

He reminded me anyway. "Slamming doors? Telling her to get lost? That's not like you, Holly. What's going on?"

"Nothing."

"Nothing? Pull the other one! You've been in a mood since the weekend."

"I don't like being bossed about, that's all," I said, staring out of the window as Dad headed towards the main road.

"Bossed about? Who by?"

"Tracie."

"Tracie? Name me one time!"

"Putting me on a diet without even asking."

"Putting you on a diet? What are you talking about?"

"I heard her in the kitchen on Saturday. Banging on about the fat content in fish and chips. Well, fish and chips *can* be fatty, but fish is really good for you and if you burn it off afterwards…" I was going to explain about Michael Phelps, but Dad didn't let me finish.

"Holly, you muppet – Tracie's not putting *you* on a diet, she's putting *me* on a diet!"

"What?"

He grunted. "I had a medical for work the other week. Basically, I'm overweight, have high cholesterol and am at risk of diabetes."

"That's not good!" I exclaimed. "In fact, that's dead bad!"

"Yeah, yeah, I know. The doctor's read me the riot act already, thanks, and so has Tracie. Don't you start nagging me as well. One woman in the house is enough."

"I know, but..."

"Seriously. It does my head in. I'm a grown-up; I can sort it."

"OK."

So that was what Tracie had wanted to talk to me about. Dad had to – I nearly thought "go on a diet", but remembered what Bev said and changed it to "start eating healthily". And I'd jumped to the wrong conclusions because ... I took a deep breath ...

because Tracie could easily have been talking about me, too. I *was* overweight and I *was* self-conscious about it. I could joke all I wanted about having chocolate-covered bones, and my team-mates could use words like "strong" and "solid", but I knew I ate the wrong things at the wrong times and didn't do enough exercise.

I glanced across at Dad's pot belly. Dad, too!

As if it were listening in, my stomach rumbled so loudly it made me jump. Dad heard it too, and laughed. "Hey! Fancy a Chinese to cheer us up?" he asked.

I was starving hungry, but I was also wary. "What about Tracie? Has she prepared anything?"

"No. I told her I'd see to us both."

"OK," I said. "Lucky Dragon, here we come."

"Excellent."

"But only if you let me choose."

This time when I carried the food over to the bench I had only one carrier bag, but the aroma coming from it was still *soooooooo* inviting.

"Where's my fried rice? And my ribs?" Dad grumbled as he lifted the foil lid on his chicken chop suey.

"You'll get spare ribs when I can see your real ribs." I grinned.

"Cheek!" He laughed and shook his head before digging into his bean shoots with a plastic fork.

After a few minutes of munching, Dad mentioned Tracie again. "She *is* trying, you know, Hols."

I felt bad for getting the whole diet thing wrong. "I know she is," I said; "and I will say sorry about telling her to get lost."

"I don't think she minded that so much."

"Didn't she?"

"No. She said it was the first time you'd shown any real emotion towards her."

"What d'you mean?"

"She sometimes feels that you treat her a bit like a guest who's outstayed her welcome. You know … polite, but wondering when she'll leave."

I couldn't deny it. It was how I felt about her most of the time.

"I mean, we do realize it's been difficult, having to share your old dad after years of it being just you and me."

"Uh-huh."

"We have tried to take it slow."

"I know."

"But there's slow and there's *slow.*"

"I know. I get it."

"So be nice."

"I'll be nice," I promised.

13

I started being nice as soon as we got back from training. I apologized to Tracie about the car-door-slamming thing and she said it didn't matter. I said it did, and explained how I'd got hold of the wrong end of the stick. Then we all sat down at the kitchen table and had the longest talk ever about food. I gabbled on and on about Bev's session and what I'd learned, and they both nodded and smiled – more at my enthusiasm than at what I was saying, I think.

Tracie made us a cup of tea and we huddled round the computer and checked out Bev's website. We downloaded loads of her recipes. "So if we cut down on the takeaways and eat these meals we'll be so much healthier." I beamed, tapping the printouts.

"Exactly!" Tracie nodded.

"Hmm," Dad said. He sounded majorly underwhelmed.

"And now that the evenings are longer, we could do more stuff at night. Like go for walks together..." I continued.

"Or cycle. I used to love cycling when I was younger," Tracie suggested.

"Yeah! Cycling. Or tennis or swimming. Anything! As long as we do *something* – especially now the season's nearly over."

"I can't see myself on a bike." Dad scowled.

"I can," I said and went to find the Argos catalogue.

From that night on, Tracie and I were a team. A help-Andy-get-fit-and-healthy team, even though I was getting fit and healthy at the same time and so was Tracie. Now that was weird. You'll never guess what? It turned out that Tracie's self-conscious thing – to add to the list of my tum, Megan's hair and Eve's feet – was that she hated being so bony. At school her nickname had been Anna Rexic, and when she was a teenager she'd stopped going out because she thought everyone was staring at her.

"Well that's just dumb!" I said. "As if it's your fault you're naturally slim. Everyone has a different body shape."

"I know that now," she said quietly, "but it took me a long time."

"Aw," I said and gave her my first proper hug.

Lauren was a bit suspicious about it all at first. "It won't last," she said, running her fingers across the railings on the way to school. "It's part of step two. A cunning part, I admit, but it's still a part."

"It's not. There are no parts, apart from the part where we get Dad into shape."

Lauren scowled at me. "And you're definitely going to the presentation evening now?"

"Uh-huh."

I'd had a big change of mind about that one,

at training the week after Bev's talk. Megan had pulled me to one side to whisper that she was starting a collection to buy Hannah and Katie a present, and asked if I wanted to contribute. I'd said yes, of course, and she was about to suggest how much when I saw Katie approaching so I had to change the subject fast.

"So ... er ... what are you wearing to the presentation evening?" Don't ask me why I asked that. I haven't a clue.

Megan frowned, giving me the sort of look she usually reserves for Amy – then when she saw Katie looming, she replied, "Jeans and my England shirt. What about you?"

"Er ... same, only Foxes shirt."

There. I'd committed myself in front of my coach and captain. I would have to go now.

"But you hate discos," Lauren now reminded me.

"I won't be dancing! I'll just be mingling."

"Mingling!"

I sighed. "I don't want to be like Tracie was,

missing out on things because I'm self-conscious."

"*I'm* self-conscious," Lauren said.

"What about? Your dyslexia?"

"No. My nutty best friend!" she whooped, giving me a shove.

I shoved her back and then darted along the path. "Race ya!" I shouted.

"As if," she shouted back – but I could hear her running.

14

It was Saturday 3 May, three weeks after the Lutton Ash match, and I awoke to the sweet chirruping of birds outside my window. I flung back my curtains, blinking as the sun streamed in. "Hello, pretty birds." I waved at them. "Hello, pretty cherry tree. Guess what today is? It's the last match of the season! And after that, the presentation evening and disco."

I joined them in a little singsong and danced round the bedroom. I caught sight of myself in the wardrobe mirror and giggled, pulling my baggy PJ bottoms up at the same time. They were looser these days.

Downstairs, I filled the kettle, warmed the teapot and prepared my breakfast. Boiled egg with buttered wholemeal toast soldiers. Nutritious and delicious. I'm a poet and I know it!

Once I'd set out my eggcup and put the bread in the toaster, ready, I took the tea up to Dad and Tracie. Tracie was sitting up in bed, looking bemused. "Wow! Thank you, Holly. This *is* a treat."

I shrugged. "Don't worry, it's a one-off," I told her, setting the tea on the bedside cabinet. I glanced round. "Where's Dad?"

"You'll never guess," she said.

"Gone to buy a paper?"

"Gone for a jog!"

"No way!"

"It's true."

"That's good," I said. "That means he's taking things seriously."

Tracie grinned. "Thanks to you!"

"Thanks to *you*."

"Thanks to us both." She took a sip of her tea. "And you're sure you're OK with me coming to watch you play?"

"Sure. Why wouldn't I be?" I said.

Having Tracie come to the match didn't seem such a big deal now. Who cared if the Mowborough lot fussed round her or if she said annoying things about the game? She was rooting for me and that's all that mattered.

She had chosen a good match to come and watch. Greenbow United were third in the league, just below the Grove Belles and the Tembridge Vixens. We were still sixth, but there were only three points separating us. A win today could make a big difference to our final positions – as Dad kept telling her.

"That is, if Hannah wises up and puts her strongest side out," he added, before launching into a long-winded description of what Hannah should and shouldn't do.

"Is he always like this?" Tracie asked me.

"Yep," I said. "I recommend earplugs."

When we reached the pitch it was obvious Greenbow wanted to celebrate the last match of the season in style. There was a Caribbean steel band pounding away and they had quite a crowd. The parents even brought round plastic cups full of home-made lemonade and gigantic chocolate-chip cookies for everybody.

"It's not always like this," I explained to Tracie, taking a cookie and putting it in my kit bag for later.

"Pity," she said, bobbing her head in time to the music.

I left her and Dad standing arm in arm and went to join my team-mates. Hannah was sitting on a camping chair, her leg resting on our heaped bags. "Just go out there and have fun, girls," was her advice before she read out the starting line-up.

She chose Petra and me for the back, with the twins on the wings, and Nika and Tabinda up front.

"I'm not scared today," Dylan told me.

"No, they're not choppy girls, this lot," I reassured her.

"And Mrs Woolcock's here for if I fall over, like at school!"

I laughed. "Yeah, she is."

☆ ☆ ☆

Do you know what? Bev was totally right about
having breakfast before a game. I was on fire!
I know that sounds really big-headed, but I was.
I was marking up and jockeying and blocking passes
left, right and centre. I felt as if I could do anything
today. The best bit was when Megan was caught out
of position and I cleared a dead cert off the goal
line. The Greenbow coach, a cheerful guy
with dreadlocks, clapped me. "Bostin' defendin',
Parrs."

"Holly, you're playing another blinder!" Hannah
told me at half-time as I scrambled for my water
bottle.

"That's 'cos I had a boiled egg and toast for
breakfast, after what Bev told us."

"Well, have two eggs when we play the Belles
next season. That's an order!"

Even if I *was* playing a blinder Hannah still brought
me off, putting Amy on in my place instead, so

I strode across to stand near Dad and Tracie for a bit.

"Now what's she done that for?" Dad chuntered.

"What?"

"Put Minto in instead of you. Terrible decision. Terrible."

"Dad. Shut up."

But as if to prove his point, Greenbow scored. Their striker, who'd been a threat all through the first half, dodged round Amy easily and side-footed the ball into the right-hand side of the net before Megan could respond. The Greenbow spectators celebrated in style, whooping and throwing ticker tape in the air.

"There you go," Dad muttered.

"We'll equalize, don't worry," I said with confidence.

And we did. Five minutes later Nika had a shot – but it hit the post. Luckily, Eve was there to gather the rebound and she blasted the ball home.

"Better!" Dad praised. "Much better."

☆ ☆ ☆

It was still one-all with about ten minutes to go. Greenbow were getting the better of us, and I could see that Amy was feeling the pressure as the ball ended up more and more in our six-yard box. Megan was bellowing instructions, but Greenbow wanted another goal and were playing flat out to get it.

Katie called me across. "Holly! Get ready to swap in for Amy."

"About time," Dad said.

"Dad! Zip it." I told him as Amy jogged towards me.

The look of relief on her face was so telling. "Finally! I thought she'd never swap me over. I need to check my texts!" she said to me.

"No you don't, you fibber – you've just had enough!"

"I'm sure I don't know what you mean." She grinned.

I homed in on their keen striker immediately,

making sure I was wherever she was. It meant I gave away throw-ins when I intercepted passes near the touchline, but at least it slowed Greenbow down and meant we had more balls played forward. Gemma had a couple of shots, but nothing came of them.

Final score: one-all.

Nika was named player of the match, but Hannah singled me out for praise as well. "Sterling defending from Holly. Sterling! And Petra, I liked the way you—"

Hannah never got a chance to finish. The Greenbow parents and players had formed a conga line and wanted us to join in. At the front was their coach, who grabbed hold of Katie, and Katie grabbed hold of me and I grabbed hold of Dylan and she grabbed Eve and so on until we were weaving all over the place. Poor Hannah was left sitting there, laughing her head off.

"Well, that was great!" Tracie said when we finally managed to escape.

A bit OTT was Dad's opinion.

"If you think that was mad, wait until tonight,"
I told him.

"Tonight?"

"Dur – keep up, Dad. The presentation evening!"

15

You know how time is really strange sometimes? Like some afternoons when you get in from school seem to stretch for ever and ever, because there's nothing on TV, and you've done all your homework, and you don't feel like reading – and you end up waiting for bedtime because you're so bored? But other evenings are so fantastic that they just go in a flash? That's what happened on the presentation evening. It went in a flash. Not even that. A supersonic flash – and that's like a million times faster than a normal flash.

One second I seemed to have only just arrived and then, before I knew it, everyone was hugging each other and saying: "Goodbye" "See you next season" "Have a great holiday!" To remember that whole, amazing event properly, I have to go on the

Parrs website and click the Under 11s page. I scroll down the fixture list and the match reports until I reach the photo gallery. Then all the pictures appear and the night is brought back to life, making my heart thud all over again.

The first shot is of us all in a group when we'd just arrived, arms round each other's shoulders, smiling at the camera. I'm at one end of the row in my Foxes shirt and Megan's at the other in her England shirt, and Amy's in the middle in her denim miniskirt, pink tights, Ugg boots, white spangly top, crimson waistcoat and perfectly straightened hair. We made her take her sunglasses off.

Then there are a few random photos of us in small groups, chatting, laughing, drinking from plastic cups and headbutting balloons.

After that come the more formal ones. Pictures taken as the awards were given out. Bev was our guest of honour, and the first one is of her with all the trophies on a table before they were awarded.

There were loads of them. It turned out we were all going to receive a prize. "Typical," Dad had tutted when Hannah made the announcement. "Everybody wins something whether they deserve it or not."

"Zip it, misery guts," Tracie had told him – beating me to it.

He was wrong, actually. If you check out that photo on the website you'll see that four of the trophies were larger than the rest – while most were palm-sized engraved shields, four were bronze statuettes of a girl in a stiff pose, her back foot positioned as if about to kick the bronze ball glued to her boot. It was obvious that even if everyone did walk away with something, some trophies were a little more special than others.

The next few photos show Bev awarding the smaller shields to Amy, Tabinda, Dylan, Eve, Jenny-Jane, Nika, Petra and Lucy.

After that come the shots of the main awards being presented. What you don't see is me with my fingers crossed for Megan. What you do see is:

☆ Bev giving the first trophy to Daisy for Most Improved Player, and Daisy, wide-eyed and speechless, almost dropping it.

☆ Bev presenting the second award to Gemma for the Coaches' Player of the Season, with Gemma's face obscured by her hair as she tries to hide her embarrassment.

☆ Bev awarding Megan with her trophy. There are two shots of this one. In the first, Megan has a ginormous grin on her face as she leans forward to shake Bev's hand, and in the second she's holding the trophy above her head. The caption on the website reads: "Megan Fawcett, Parsnips' captain, receives the prestigious award for 'Clubman' – the one who has contributed most to the club. Quite right too – who could have contributed more than our Meggo?"

☆ And finally, Bev presenting me with the award for the Players' Player of the Season. Yes, me! Even now I can't believe it – I still have to keep going to the website, even though I've got the trophy on my dressing table at home to prove I won.

In the picture of me receiving the statuette I look exactly like Daisy did when she received hers: wide-eyed and speechless – but maybe a bit more overwhelmed. The caption reads: "Holly Woolcock receiving the trophy for the Players' Player of the Season. Why she should look so surprised we don't know. Among the reasons her team-mates gave for nominating her were: 'She always explains things to me if I'm stuck' (Nika); 'We work well together at the back' (Lucy); 'She so gets me' (Amy); 'Hollybolly saves me from the highly mean girls' (Dylan); 'I feel better knowing she's alongside me in defence' (Petra); 'She is super-reliable – plus I wasn't allowed to vote for Petra!' (Megan). So well done, Wonder. Awesome!"

"I thought you said defenders never win," I said to Dad afterwards as I showed him the trophy.

"Well, there's always the exception that proves the rule." He sniffed, wiping his eyes with a hanky.

I peered closer. "Dad, are you crying?"

"Men call it hay fever," Tracie whispered.

Then the website photos become more informal again. Ones with us crowding round Hannah and Katie when we presented them with enormous bouquets of flowers. Ones of us all dancing to "Here Come the Girls". Ones of us all enjoying ourselves, whatever shape or size we were. Ones of us, the Parrs Under 11s. The best girls' team on the planet.

Final Whistle

Well, that's my bit over and done with already. As you can see, we stayed sixth in the league at the end, with 29 points – but I think that's pretty decent for a first season, don't you?

Team	P	W	D	L	Pts
Grove Belles	18	16	1	1	49
Tembridge Vixens	18	12	1	5	37
Greenbow United Girls	18	10	3	5	33
Furnston Diamonds	18	9	3	6	30
Misslecott Goldstars	18	9	3	6	30
Parrs U11s	18	9	2	7	29
Cuddlethorpe Tigers	18	6	3	9	21
Hixton Lees Juniors	18	3	7	8	16
Lutton Ash Angels	18	2	1	15	7
Southfields Athletic	18	1	2	15	5

Looking back, if I were to pick out my highlight, it wouldn't be when I won the Players' Player of the Season award, brilliant though that was. It would be when Megan dragged me out of the toilet (well, not out of the toilet *itself*, but you know what I mean). If she hadn't done that, I would have missed Bev's talk, and Bev's talk changed my life.

Without it, I'd still be missing meals before matches and training, then ending up starving and stuffing myself silly afterwards.

Most important of all, I wouldn't be racing Dad and Tracie along Saddlebridge Common every weekend on my new bike. Cycling's nearly as good as playing football. It gives you such a head rush when you go fast down a slope – though Dad's still not convinced.

I could go on and on about recipes
and body shapes and feeling self-
conscious, but if I did I'd use up
all Nika's space and that wouldn't
be fair. She's going to tell you all
about when some of the Parsnips took
part in a seven-a-side World Cup
competition over the summer. They
stayed at a holiday camp and had to
share chalets and everything. Cool or
what! I would have loved to go with
them, but the date clashed with our
summer holiday in Italy. Shame.

So I'd better be off. Goodbye, my
friends (in Italian that would be
arrivederci amici miei).

Until next season (*alla prossima
stagione*).

Except you, Smelly Shell (*tranne te,
Smellyo Shellyo*).

Holly Wonder xxxx